TREE·MAN

TREE·MAN

Carmen Agra Deedy

Illustrated by Douglas J. Ponte

PEACHTREE PUBLISHERS, LTD.

Atlanta

For Angela Beasley and her Puppet People
for inspiring TREEMAN;
my sister Tersi Bendiburg, a woman of
grace and strength and my hero;
my old friends, Ruthann Hendrickson and
Don Greene, Jr., a.k.a. Ana and Bill — I love you both;
and my Mami and Papi for making life an adventure.

Special thanks to Tyler Butler, Allan Hamilton, Mike Lovin,
Avis Fox, and Joe White.

Tremendous gratitude to MQ
for her inspirational editing and vision.

Published by
PEACHTREE PUBLISHERS, LTD.
494 Armour Circle NE
Atlanta, Georgia 30324

Mixed media illustrations rendered in watercolor,
colored pencil, oil pastels, and cut paper.

First printing September 1993
10 9 8 7 6 5 4 3 2 1

MANUFACTURED IN MEXICO

Library of Congress Cataloging-in-Publication Data

Deedy, Carmen Agra.
    Treeman / by Carmen Agra Deedy : illustrated by Douglas J. Ponte.
        p.   cm.
    Summary: Three jungle animal friends with a love of trees have an unexpected Christmas "happening."
    ISBN 1-56145-077-4
    [1. Jungle animals—Fiction. 2. Trees—Fiction. 3. Christmas—Fiction.]   I. Ponte, Douglas J., ill.   II. Title.
PZ7.D3587Tr   1993
[E]—dc20   93-1667
                                                                                                                    CIP
                                                                                                                    AC

In a dwindling forest,
deep and old,
by the banks of a river,
dark and gold,
there live three friends:

a boa named Ana Conda,
a sloth named Slow Jim,
and a toucan named Bill, just Bill.

The three friends shared a breezy, sprawling tree by the river. From there they could look out into the forest they loved: the red-berried fire trees, the fragrant jacaranda trees, and the cheery banana-yellow of the balsam pear trees.

The *tree* amigos loved the trees in their forest more than anything else, except each other.

It was practically paradise.

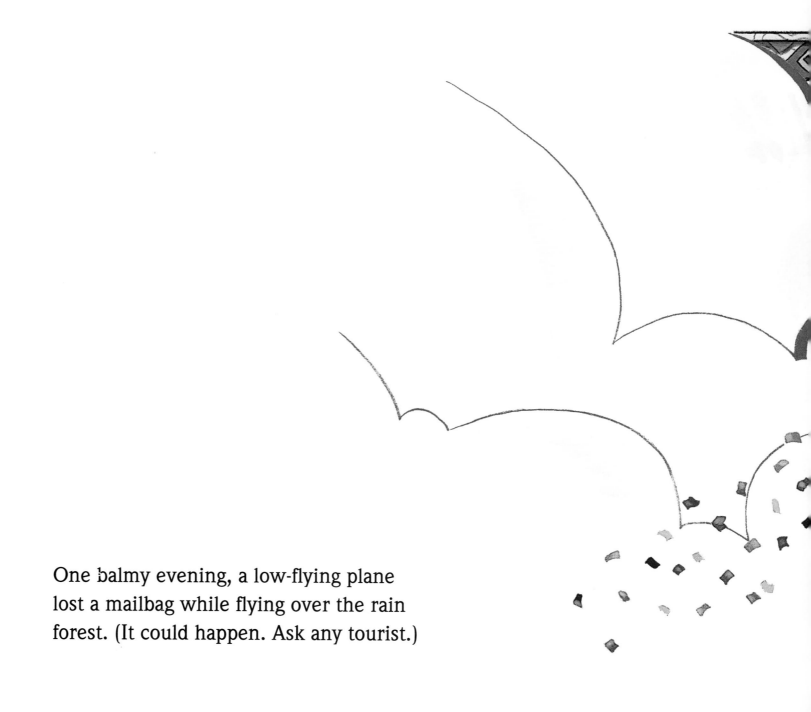

One balmy evening, a low-flying plane lost a mailbag while flying over the rain forest. (It could happen. Ask any tourist.)

Ana Conda, Slow Jim and Bill, just Bill, watched in wonder as their sky blazed with color. The cards and letters fluttered to the forest below, and one landed right on Bill's bill. You and I would have recognized it as a Christmas card. But to our friends (who had never heard of Christmas or You-Know-Who), it was a total enigma.

And that means it was very puzzling.

The three friends gathered around the fallen card and stared
at the picture of BIG RED. He had presents piled high
around his feet and his left arm rested on the most
unusual tree they had ever seen.

"What could it mean?" asked Ana Conda.

"Would you look at that fruit!" said Slow Jim.

Bill said nothing at first, then suddenly, his eyes widening,
he slapped himself on the bill and proclaimed, "Compadres,
I have it! It is as obvious as the bill on my face. You leave
this fellow presents and he leaves you . . . a tree.

I believe, my friends, that this is the TREEMAN!"

At first, Ana Conda and Slow Jim were speechless.

Jim was the first to speak.

"Are you sure you are not barking up the wrong tree, hermano?" he asked.

"You know, if Bill is right, I'd love a tree like that," said Ana Conda dreamily. "It's greener than any tree in our forest."

"And would you look at that fruit!" Slow Jim added.

Bill, just Bill, wasn't listening. He was watching the smoke rise at the edge of his beloved forest.

"This card did not just fall from the sky," said Bill, waving the Christmas card emphatically. Ana and Jim listened politely as they watched Bill pace back and forth, out on a limb.

"This TREEMAN comes when we need him most! Just when our own trees are disappearing—"

"—you think the TREEMAN would bring us one of those trees?" Ana wondered, and her eyes brightened as she looked at the Christmas card.

"I don't know," said Bill. "What could we leave *him?*"

"Why do we have to leave him anything?" asked Ana archly.

"Why Ana. How could we take such a splendid gift and not leave anything in return?" said Jim softly.

So the three friends agreed that they would leave presents for the TREEMAN. Each would select a gift from among his or her most prized possessions. And like the three kings of long ago they went in search of their offerings.

Bill, just Bill, flew through the forest and
paid a visit to his fine-feathered friends.
Ana Conda slithered off in search of succulent fruit.
And Slow Jim just hung around and thought.

That night they presented their gifts for the TREEMAN:
Ana Conda offered her precious hat. Bill, just Bill,
left a bit of himself in a feathered boa. Slow Jim
gave the shirt off his back (because he's that type of guy).

Carefully they tacked the card to their tree. In a corner, they left this message:

Dear TREEMAN,

Please leave a tree for us like the one in this picture. Muchas gracias.

Your tree amigos,
Ana Conda, Slow Jim and Bill, just Bill.

Then the friends tried to settle down for the night.

"I'm too excited to sleep," whispered Slow Jim.

"Jim, be quiet or you'll scare him away," hissed Ana.

"Morning will come much sooner if you two would just go to sleep," suggested Bill helpfully. The three were soon lulled by the sound of the raindrops in the forest.

When they awoke the next morning their gifts were gone. In their place was a very exotic tree.

"Would you look at that fruit!" exclaimed Slow Jim, reaching for a sample to taste. "Pthew!" He spit out the first bite.

"Things always look different in the catalog, Jim," said Ana Conda, wisely. "Don't you agree, Bill?"

But Bill, just Bill, wasn't listening. His eyes wandered from the prickly little fir to the lush trees all around him. "Not quite what I expected, but lovely," he muttered to himself.

As the inky smoke spiraled in the distance, Ana looked up sharply, "What about the other trees, Bill?"

Jim, who had been sprucing up the little fir, looked to Bill expectantly. Bill, just Bill, sat very still on his perch and thought. As usual, Ana and Jim waited patiently for their friend.

"One tree at a time, amigos," he finally replied.

"One tree at a time," echoed Ana with satisfaction.

"Mango. I think I'd like a mango tree next," chimed Jim hopefully as they retreated with their new tree deep into the forest they loved. It was *still* practically paradise.

One balmy evening a pilot dropped a parcel . . .

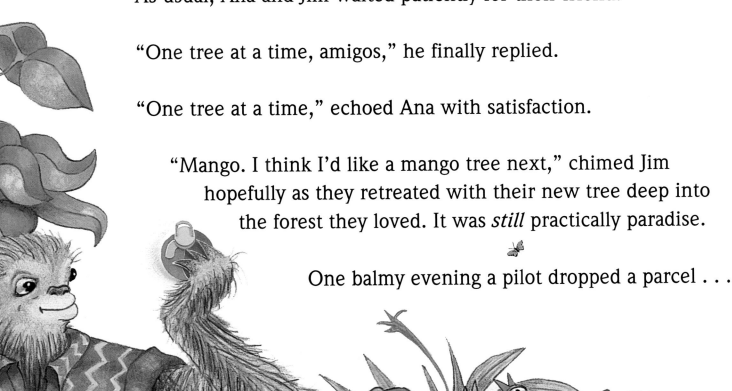

The mysterious message on the photograph read,

Dear muchachos and Señorita,

*Thanks, thanks, thanks! No one ever thinks of leaving presents for **me**.*

Your friend,
Nicholas

P.S. Have you given a thought to next year? Mango perhaps?

Dear muchachos and Señorita,
Thanks, thanks, thanks! No one ever thinks
of leaving presents for mé.   Your friend —
P.S. Have you given a thought   Nicholas
to next year? Mango perhaps?

Author's Note

Some of the world's greatest visionaries have stumbled onto their discoveries through gross miscalculation and faulty deduction. Ana Conda, Slow Jim, and Bill are just such unlikely heroes— they summed up two plus two and got five.

Children know what is crucial in heroes: not the triumph, or the defeat. What matters is the *spirit* that guides, inspires, and compels.

The result of our tree amigos' quirky logic and heroic spirit is that their forest gained not only a tree, but a Protector—the TREEMAN. And as for the TREEMAN, after a lifetime of unselfish stewardship over the world's children, he is delighted to discover *he* has presents.

Replanting one tree can change a forest; fostering this heroic spirit can change the world.

About the Author

Carmen Agra Deedy was born in Havana and grew up in Decatur, Georgia, the daughter of Cuban exiles. She has charmed thousands of children and adults as a professional storyteller, and currently contributes regular commentary to National Public Radio's "All Things Considered." Founder of the Atlanta Storytelling Festival and a frequent speaker to educators, she is the author of the popular children's book, AGATHA'S FEATHER BED: *Not Just Another Wild Goose Story,* also published by Peachtree. She lives in Tucker, Georgia, with her husband and three daughters.

About the Illustrator

Douglas J. Ponte, an illustrator and graphic designer, holds a degree in fine arts from the Pratt Institute in New York. He completed further design studies in Tokyo, Japan. In addition to his full-time work as senior designer in a corporate communications department in Atlanta, he has illustrated and designed books and promotional materials for, among others, Peachtree Publishers and the Atlanta Storytelling Festival. TREEMAN is his first children's book.